P9-DGW-078

WELCOME TO MY COUNTRY

Welcome to AUSTRIA

Gareth Stevens Publishing
A WORLD ALMANAC EDUCATION GROUP COMPANY

Written by
RONALD TAN

Edited by
KATHARINE BROWN-CARPENTER

Edited in USA by
JENETTE DONOVAN GUNTLY

Designed by
BENSON TAN

Picture research by
THOMAS KHOO
JOSHUA ANG

First published in North America in 2006 by
Gareth Stevens Publishing
A WRC Media Company
330 West Olive Street, Suite 100
Milwaukee, Wisconsin 53212 USA

Please visit our web site at
www.garethstevens.com
For a free color catalog describing
Gareth Stevens Publishing's list of high-quality
books and multimedia programs,
call 1-800-542-2595 (USA) or
1-800-387-3178 (Canada).
Gareth Stevens Publishing's fax: (414) 332-3567.

All rights reserved. No parts of this book may be reproduced or
utilized in any form or by any means, electronic or mechanical,
including photocopying, recording, or by an information storage and
retrieval system, without permission from the copyright owner.

© **MARSHALL CAVENDISH INTERNATIONAL (ASIA)**
PRIVATE LIMITED 2005
Originated and designed by
Times Editions—Marshall Cavendish
An imprint of Marshall Cavendish International (Asia) Pte Ltd
A member of Times Publishing Limited
Times Centre, 1 New Industrial Road
Singapore 536196
http://www.marshallcavendish.com/genref

Library of Congress Cataloging-in-Publication Data
Tan, Ronald.
Welcome to Austria / Ronald Tan.
p. cm. — (Welcome to my country)
Includes bibliographical references and index.
ISBN 0-8368-3133-0 (lib. bdg.)
1. Austria — Juvenile literature. I. Title. II. Series.
DB17.T36   2005
943.6—dc22   2004065358

Printed in Singapore

1 2 3 4 5 6 7 8 9 09 08 07 06 05

PICTURE CREDITS
Agence France Presse: 12, 17, 35
ANA Press Agency: 3 (top and bottom), 7,
    14, 20, 31 (bottom), 32, 33, 38, 39 (top)
Art Directors & TRIP Photo Library: 2, 4, 9,
    16, 21 (bottom), 24, 25, 34
Bettmann/Corbis: 13 (bottom), 15 (bottom)
Focus Team—Italy: 37, 40, 41
Getty Images/Hulton Archive: 10, 11,
    13 (top)
Arici Graziano/Corbis Sygma: 29
Haga Library Inc.: cover
Hans Hayden: 19
International Photobank: 5, 6, 8, 18,
    21 (top), 22, 26, 28, 30, 31 (top),
    39 (bottom), 45
Lonely Planet Images: 27
Neusiedler See Tourism/Mike Ranz:
    3 (center)
Nobel Foundation/Corbis: 15 (top)
Travel Ink: 1, 23, 36
Topham Picturepoint: 15 (center)

Digital Scanning by Superskill Graphics Pte Ltd

Contents

Words that appear in the glossary are printed in **boldface** type the first time they occur in the text.

4

Welcome to Austria!

The **Republic** of Austria is located in the center of Europe. It is known for its beautiful forests and for the Alps, a mountain chain covering large areas of the country. Austria is also known for its rich **culture**, including music, art, and architecture. Let's visit Austria and learn about its history and people!

Opposite: Many Austrian children enjoy skiing in the Eastern Alps during the winter.

Below: A couple walks along a mountain road on Grossglockner, the highest mountain in Austria.

The Flag of Austria

The flag of Austria is made up of bands of red, white, and red. The nation has two flags. Austria's citizens use the plain striped flag. The government uses a flag with Austria's official symbol, a black eagle, in the middle.

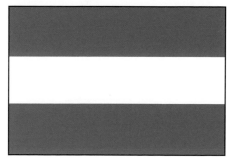

The Land

Austria has an area of 32,377 square miles (83,857 square kilometers). The country is surrounded by land on all sides. The Eastern Alps run through the western and southern parts of Austria. The Alps are part of a mountain chain that stretches across nine countries. The highest peak in Austria, Grossglockner, is in the Hohe Tauern Mountains. The peak stands 12,461 feet (3,798 meters) high. Austria's northern and eastern lands are mostly hills and plains.

Left: Mountains cover about two-thirds of Austria. All of the country's mountains are part of the Eastern Alps mountain chain.

Left: This lake in the state of Tyrol is an ideal place for fishing. Lakes are popular vacation spots for Austrians during the summer.

Rivers and Lakes

Austria's longest and most important river is the Danube River. It flows through Austria for about 220 miles (350 kilometers). The Danube River is Europe's second-longest river. Almost all of Austria's smaller rivers, including the Salzach, Drava, Enns, and Mur Rivers, drain into the Danube River.

Lake Constance and Neusiedler Lake are Austria's largest lakes. Neusiedler Lake is also Austria's lowest point.

Left:
Winters in Austria can be very cold. Temperatures in the winter usually range from about 12° Fahrenheit (-11° Celsius) in the mountains to about 30° F (-1° C) in the lowlands and in eastern Austria.

Climate

The climate in Austria is different in different regions of the country. In northwestern and western Austria, the climate is mild and wet. Southern Austria's climate is warmer than in other parts of the country. The climate in eastern Austria is cool and dry.

Sometimes, winds known as *foehn* (fayn) blow through the Austrian Alps from the south. The foehn are warm and dry and can raise temperatures rapidly. If the foehn blow during winter, they melt snow quickly, causing **avalanches**.

Plants and Animals

Almost one-fourth of Austria's land is used for nature **reserves** and parkland. Forests cover almost half of Austria's land. Trees in these forests include oak, spruce, beech, fir, larch, and stone pine.

Austria has many kinds of animals, including marten, brown bears, ibex, red deer, marmots, and chamois. Many kinds of birds, including purple herons and avocets, live near Neusiedler Lake. Fish, such as carp, rainbow trout, and perch, live in the country's many rivers.

Left: The edelweiss flower grows high up in the mountains of Austria.

History

Human settlers lived in the area that is now Austria thousands of years ago, but very little is known about them. In 400 B.C., Celtic tribes took over what is now central and southern Austria and named it Noricum. The Romans took control of the region in 15 B.C. They ruled for the next five hundred years.

In A.D. 976, the Babenberg **dynasty** began its rule over Austria. Babenberg rule ended in 1246 when the last ruler, Frederick II, died without an **heir**.

Left: This painting shows the crowning of Charlemagne (*left*), king of the Franks, in A.D. 774. He took control of what is now Austria during the 700s.

The Habsburgs

In 1282, the Holy Roman **emperor**, Rudolf von Habsburg, gave his two sons control of Austria. The Habsburgs took control of most of Austria and also parts of Germany, France, Italy, Croatia, and Slovenia. Because the Habsburgs gained power over land through marriages to powerful people, they became known as the House of Austria. The Habsburgs ruled their lands for about six hundred years.

Above:
Charles I was the last Habsburg ruler of Austria. He ruled for only three years before he and his family were forced to leave the country in 1919.

The Powerful Habsburg Empire

By the 1500s, the Habsburg Empire was at the height of its power. In the 1700s and 1800s, the Habsburgs began to lose power. In 1867, the empire was divided into two regions. Together, the regions were called Austria-Hungary or the Austro-Hungarian Empire. In 1914, Archduke Franz Ferdinand, Austria's heir to the throne, and his wife visited Bosnia, where they were both killed. Austria-Hungary then declared war on Serbia. Other nations joined the fight, which grew to become World War I.

Left:
Archduke Franz Ferdinand and his wife, Sophie, were killed on June 28, 1914. They were killed by a group that wanted Bosnia to leave the Austro-Hungarian Empire and join with Serbia.

Left: In Vienna, a group of Jews was forced to scrub the pavement as Nazi soldiers watched. By the end of World War II, about 65,000 Austrian Jews had been murdered in Nazi **concentration camps**. In all, about 81,000 Austrians died in the camps.

World Wars

During World War I, Austria-Hungary fought alongside Germany and Turkey. They were defeated in 1918. In 1919, the Habsburg Empire ended. Its lands were divided into separate nations. The Republic of Austria was one of them.

In 1938, Nazi Germany took control of Austria, and Adolf Hitler joined the countries together. The Germans and Austrians fought other countries to gain power, leading to World War II. More than 247,000 Austrian soldiers died.

Below: *The Sound of Music*, a popular musical and movie, is based on the true story of the Trapp family. They were able to escape from Nazi-ruled Austria. In all, about 130,000 people left Austria during that time.

Austria after the War

In 1945, Germany was defeated, and Austria became a republic again. Under the control of the Allies, the nations that worked together to win World War II, Austria became a **democratic** country.

In 1955, the Allies left and gave full control back to Austria. That same year, Austria became neutral, meaning it does not take sides with other countries. As a neutral nation, Austria has helped other nations solve problems. Austria joined the European Union (EU) in 1995.

Left: In 1979, a new **United Nations** (UN) headquarters, one of only three in the world, was built in Vienna. Austria was accepted into the UN in 1955 and has since been part of many important UN groups.

Bertha von Suttner (1843–1914)

A great supporter of peace, Bertha von Suttner influenced many people with her writing, especially her novel about war. Alfred Nobel is believed to have created the Nobel Peace Prize because of her. In 1905, Bertha was given the prize for her work in support of peace.

Bertha von Suttner

Ignaz Seipel (1876–1932)

Ignaz Seipel was a Catholic priest who became Austria's **chancellor** from 1922 to 1924 and from 1926 to 1929. He helped improve Austria's economy by getting a $100 million loan from the League of Nations, a group set up by the Allies during World War I.

Ignaz Seipel

Bruno Kreisky (1911–1990)

During the 1930s, Bruno Kreisky was put in jail several times for his political views. From 1970 to 1983, he served as Austria's chancellor. During his time in office, he helped Austria gain respect through its role as a neutral country.

Bruno Kreisky

Government and the Economy

The **federal** president is Austria's head of state, or official public leader. The president chooses a cabinet, which is a group of advisers, and also chooses the federal chancellor, who is in charge of the nation's government.

The National Council is one part of Austria's **parliament**. The council has 183 elected members. It is the nation's main lawmaking group.

Below: The Austrian parliament building is located in Vienna, the capital city of Austria. Vienna is considered both a city and a state, so the city's mayor also serves as the state's **governor**.

Left: Members of the National Council are elected to office by Austrian citizens. All Austrians age nineteen or older can vote.

The Federal Council is the second part of Austria's parliament. It is made up of sixty-two members. The council meets to talk about issues regarding the country's nine states, which are called *Länder* (LEN-der). The states are Tyrol, Burgenland, Lower Austria, Carinthia, Salzburg, Vorarlberg, Upper Austria, Styria, and Vienna.

Each of Austria's nine states has its own state government and is headed by a governor and deputies. Each state also has a *Landtag* (LAHND-tahg), or land parliament, which passes state laws.

Left: Many Austrian shops sell locally made crafts. Many crafts are sold to tourists. Tourism is a very important industry in Austria.

The Economy

Most Austrians live very well because Austria is one of the wealthiest nations in the EU. Austria's government owns one-fourth of the country's companies, including heavy industries, such as steel manufacturing, and public services, such as telephone companies.

More than half of all Austrians have service jobs, such as in tourism. Many people also have jobs in industries, including food processing. Another important Austrian industry is making crafts, such as jewelry and glass items.

Natural Resources

Austria has many natural resources, including **minerals** such as lead, iron, and white gold. Austria is the world's largest producer of magnesite, a mineral used in the nation's chemical industry. Steel and iron are used in industries, such as car making, and are **exported**.

Because almost half of the country is covered in forests, cutting timber and making wood products, such as paper, are important industries in Austria.

Austria produces energy by mining fuels, such as natural gas and coal, and by producing **hydroelectric** power.

Left: Fresh produce grown in Austria is sold in markets all over the country. Austria produces fruits, grains, wine, and potatoes.

People and Lifestyle

Most people in Austria are German. Small numbers of Croats, Hungarians, Czechs, Slovaks, Slovenes, and Roma also live in the country. In the middle to late 1900s, a large number of Eastern Europeans moved to Austria. Most of the people in Austria live in the eastern regions of the country on lower land, where it is warmer. About one-fifth of all Austrians live in the city of Vienna.

Below: Food and drink are poured over men as part of the fun during a winter carnival held in the city of Telfs.

The Austrian Way of Life

Austrians enjoy drinking coffee at cafés and watching people go by. They also enjoy spending time with their families and friends. This relaxed enjoyment of life is called *Gemuetlichkeit* (GEH-moot-lihk-EYET) in Austria.

Some Austrians own vacation homes, mostly in the countryside. People often visit their vacation homes on weekends and holidays. Some people spend their vacations at farms that offer activities such as horseback riding or fishing.

Above: In Austria, family and friends often enjoy sharing meals outdoors.

Above: Vacationing at a farm is popular with both Austrians and tourists. Austria has more than three thousand farms that people can visit.

Families

Most Austrian families are small, with only one or two children. Because city living is expensive, most people living in cities have fewer children than those living in the countryside.

Since the 1970s, the divorce rate in Austria has been rising. In 2002, almost half of all marriages in Austria ended in divorce. Since the 1960s, the number of single-parent families also has gone up in Austria.

Austrian Women

In Austria, many women stay at home and take care of their households while their husbands work. More and more women are getting jobs outside of the home, however. Because these women want to have careers, many of them are getting married and having children at a later age. Although Austrian women have the same rights as Austrian men, women are often paid less than men are for doing the same work.

Above: Single-parent families are more common in Austria today than in the past.

Opposite: A mother and her children sit and feed swans by a lake. In Austria, the government gives paid time off and free medical care to women after they have had babies.

23

Education

Austrian children must attend school from age six to age fifteen. They must attend *Volksschule* (FOLK-schoo-luh), or elementary school, for four years. At age eleven, students choose either a four-year middle school or an eight-year secondary school. Secondary schools prepare students to attend universities and teach subjects such as mathematics, music, art, and science.

Left: Skiing is one of the sports taught during physical education classes in Austrian schools. Students must take physical education classes from the first to the twelfth year of school.

Schools of Higher Learning

After completing middle school or secondary school, students may attend a school of higher learning, such as a **vocational** school, a military academy, a teacher training school, or a music school. Students who have completed secondary school and who have earned a *Reifeprüfung* (REYE-feh-PROO-foong), or diploma, may attend one of Austria's nineteen universities.

Above:
The University of Vienna is Austria's oldest and largest university. It was founded in 1365 by Rudolf IV. The university is well known around the world for turning out great students, including nine people who went on to win Nobel Prizes.

Religion

Christianity came to Austria during the second century A.D. In the 1500s, the Habsburgs forced people in Austria and all over the empire to become Catholic. Today, Austrians may choose their own religions, but most people in Austria are still Catholic. The Catholic Church used to be very powerful in Austrian society. Now, however, few Austrians attend church regularly. Many Catholics only attend church on holidays.

Below: These Roman Catholics are celebrating a Christian holiday called Corpus Christi in a town near Salzburg.

Left: This **memorial** was built in Upper Austria. It stands at the Mauthausen Concentration Camp. It honors the thousands of Jews in Austria who were killed by the Nazis during World War II.

During the 1500s, many Austrians became Protestants, but the Habsburgs forced them to become Catholics. Even today, few Austrians are Protestants. Some Muslims, who are followers of the Islamic religion, live in Austria.

In 1938, about 200,000 Jews lived in Austria, but about half of them fled the country. After World War II began, thousands of Austrian Jews were taken prisoner and killed by Nazis. Today, only about 7,000 Jews live in Austria.

Language

Austria's official language is German. Most Austrians speak German. Many Austrians also speak local languages that are similar to German. The local languages sound different from region to region. To talk to people in different areas of the country, most Austrians speak *Hochdeutsch* (hoch-DOYTCH), or High German. It is also sometimes called standard German. Hochdeutsch was first spoken in the mountain areas of Austria, Germany, and Switzerland.

Left: Two women in **traditional** Austrian costumes stop to talk during a local festival. Although German is Austria's official language, many people speak local languages.

Left: Peter Handke is a well-known Austrian writer. His most famous work is *The Goalie's Anxiety at the Penalty Kick* (1970).

Literature

Starting in the 1100s, most literature written in Austria was poetry about religion or the Habsburg rulers. During the 1700s, Austrian literature and arts began to grow. The Austro-Hungarian Empire ended in 1918. Karl Kraus and Joseph Roth wrote about how unsure Austrians felt during that time. After World War II, Thomas Bernhard wrote about the suffering, deaths, and social wrongs in Austria. Today, well-known Austrian authors include Ilse Aichinger and Ingeborg Bachmann.

Arts

Austria is famous around the world for its architecture and art. The country is also famous for its music.

Architecture

Austria is very well known for its many **cathedrals**. In the 1500s, the **baroque** style became popular. Many cathedrals and palaces were built in this style. In the 1600s, architect Johann Bernhard Fischer von Erlach created the Austrian baroque style, which mixes the baroque style with other styles of architecture.

Left: St. Stephen's Cathedral was first built in Vienna in the 1100s. Later, it was rebuilt in the gothic style. The gothic style uses pointy arches, such as can be seen on top of the windows of St. Stephen's.

Left: A street artist is using chalk to draw a portrait of a woman on a sidewalk in the city of Innsbruck.

In the 1800s, Austrian Adolf Loos created a simple style of architecture. It influenced modern European styles. Today, Coop Himmelblau and Hans Hollein are famous Austrian architects.

Above: This colorful building in Vienna combines modern art and architecture.

Painting

Gustav Klimt is one of Austria's most famous artists. In 1897, he formed a group called the Vienna Sezession. The group's styles of art led to the modern styles used by later artists, such as Egon Schiele and Oskar Kokoschka.

Music

Some of the greatest **composers** in the world come from Austria. The most famous Austrian composer is Wolfgang Amadeus Mozart (1756–1791). He wrote many pieces of music, including forty-one **symphonies**. Joseph Haydn (1732–1809) is also very famous. He is known for his music and for teaching Ludwig van Beethoven (1770–1827), a famous German composer.

Left: A boy plays a violin on a street in Vienna. Joseph Haydn is famous for his music and for creating the string quartet, a group of four musicians. The musicians play two violins, a cello, and a viola.

Austrian composer Johann Strauss the Younger wrote *The Blue Danube* (1867). It is a famous waltz, which is a style of music that started in Austria. The waltz is also a dance. Waltz music and dancing became very popular in Austria and all of Europe in the 1800s.

Many Austrian composers also have written music for the theater. Mozart wrote sixteen **operas**, including *Don Giovanni*. Johann Strauss the Younger wrote operettas, or funny operas with both talking and singing.

Above: The Vienna Opera House is well known for hosting some of Austria's best music groups. The famous Vienna Philharmonic Orchestra often plays at the Vienna Opera House. An orchestra is a large group of musicians who play pieces of music together.

Leisure

Most Austrians enjoy sports, including swimming, skiing, horseback riding, tennis, soccer, and golf. These activities help Austrians relax and stay healthy.

During the summertime, hiking and climbing in the mountains are popular activities. Austria has many trails for hikers. Riding bicycles in the mountains is also popular. A cycling race called the Tour d'Autriche is held every year. The race travels 930 miles (1,500 km) through Austria's mountains.

Left: Sunbathing at a lake is a popular summer activity in Austria. Austria has many lakes, and swimming is one of the country's most popular sports.

Left:
In 1984, Thomas Muster became Austria's national tennis champion. He was seventeen years old. In 1996, he was ranked the world's top male tennis player.

Sports Competitions

Austria has many athletes who perform well in sports competitions with other nations. Niki Lauda, a famous Austrian racecar driver, became the Formula One racing champion in 1975, 1977, and 1984. In 1984 and 1988, Austria's Peter Seisenbacher won Olympic medals in judo. At the 2000 Summer Olympics in Sydney, Australia, the Austrians won two gold medals in sailing.

Winter Sports

Skiing is one of Austria's most popular winter activities. Many people vacation at ski resorts in Austria during winter. In fact, the style of downhill skiing used around the world today was invented in Austria. Many Austrians enjoy snow boarding, sledding, and ice-skating, too.

Austria is one of the world's leading skiing nations. Since 1924, Austrians have won more than forty gold medals in the Winter Olympics.

Left: These children are ice-skating in the square in front of Vienna's City Hall. During the winter, the square is filled with water so that it can become an ice-skating rink.

Left: Viennese coffeehouses have been popular places to visit for hundreds of years. Austrians go to coffeehouses not only to drink coffee, but also to relax, watch people go by, play chess, read, visit friends, and write poetry.

Social Life in Austria

Social life in Austria is relaxed. Many Austrians visit parks or forests in the summer. At night, beer gardens and *Heurigen* (HOY-rih-GEHN), or wine taverns, are popular places to meet. At wine taverns, Austrians taste local wines, visit with friends, and eat meals. The most popular places to gather are Viennese coffeehouses. Austrians often spend many hours at coffeehouses.

Holidays and Festivals

Many holidays celebrated in Austria are religious. On Palm Sunday, the Sunday before Easter, Austrian Catholics attend church. They have their *Palmkätzchen* (palm-KETZ-chen) blessed by priests. Palmkätzchen, or braided pussy-willow branches, are symbols of rebirth. On Christmas Eve, Austrian adults decorate Christmas trees, but the children are not allowed to see. After Christmas dinner, a bell is rung to declare that the Christ-child has come, bringing them presents.

Left: These men are wearing costumes and masks during a *Fasching* (fah-SHING) parade in Tyrol. Fasching is the time between the holidays of the Epiphany and Ash Wednesday. Some Austrians in Tyrol believe that wearing masks during the time of Fasching scares away the evil spirits of winter.

Left: This couple is waltzing at a waltz festival. The waltz is a popular ballroom dance in Austria.

Many Austrian festivals celebrate the country's culture. During Fasching, many Austrians attend ballroom dances. They dress in fancy dresses and suits or in *Trachten* (TRAHK-tun), which are the traditional clothes of Austria.

Each summer, the Salzburg Festival is held in Salzburg. It lasts for five to six weeks and is Austria's best-known arts festival. During this event, many world-class operas, plays, and concerts are performed.

Below: This man and woman are wearing Trachten. The women's outfits are called the *Dirndl* (DEERN-dl). Most of the men wear pairs of leather shorts called *Lederhosen* (LAY-duh-HOH-zun).

Food

Austrian food has been influenced by German, Czech, Italian, and Hungarian foods. Common Austrian foods include meat, dumplings, and fish. The country is well known for its Viennese cooking, especially cakes, pastries, and *Wiener Backhendel* (VEE-nah BAHK-hayn-dl), or Viennese fried chicken. Two favorite Austrian dishes are *Knödel* (NOH-del), or stuffed dumplings, and *Tafelspitz* (TAH-fehl-SPEETZ), or boiled beef.

Left: The *Wiener schnitzel* (VEE-nah SHNIT-zel) is a traditional Austrian meat dish. It is a fried piece of veal. Sometimes, pork or turkey is used instead of veal.

Apfelstrudel (ahp-FEHL-stroo-dehl), or apple strudel, is a famous Austrian dessert. It is a baked pastry filled with apples and raisins. A rich chocolate cake called the *Sachertorte* (SAH-kehr-TOHR-teh) is also famous. The recipe is kept secret at Vienna's Hotel Sacher. At Christmastime, Christmas fruit bread and other homemade treats are popular.

Austrian adults usually drink beer or wine with meals. Austrians living near Germany usually drink beer, not wine.

Above: Vienna's desserts, including tortes and strudel, are famous around the world. Tortes are rich cakes made from chopped nuts and eggs with little or no flour. Often, tortes and strudel are served with coffee at Viennese coffeehouses.

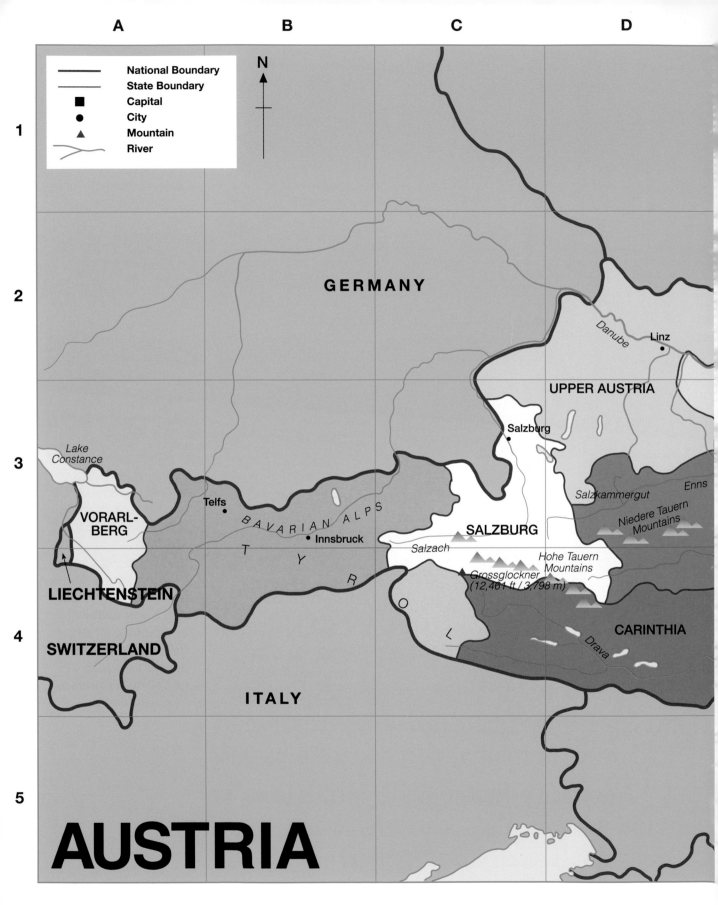

A | B | C | D

1

2

GERMANY

Danube

Linz

UPPER AUSTRIA

3

Lake Constance

Salzburg

VORARL-
BERG

Telfs

B A V A R I A N   A L P S

Salzkammergut

Enns

SALZBURG

Niedere Tauern Mountains

T
Y
R
O
L

Innsbruck

Salzach

Hohe Tauern
Mountains

Grossglockner
(12,461 ft / 3,798 m)

LIECHTENSTEIN

4

SWITZERLAND

CARINTHIA

Drava

ITALY

5

AUSTRIA

Legend:
National Boundary
State Boundary
■ Capital
● City
▲ Mountain
River

N

E	F

CZECH REPUBLIC

LOWER AUSTRIA

Danube Valley

Danube

■ *VIENNA*
VIENNA

Neusiedler Lake

SLOVAKIA

STYRIA

Mur

BURGENLAND

• Graz

HUNGARY

SLOVENIA

CROATIA

Bavarian Alps
    B3–C3
Burgenland (state)
    F2–F4

Carinthia (state)
    C4–E4
Croatia E5–F5
Czech Republic
    C1–F2

Danube River A2–F3
Drava River C4–F5

Enns River D3–E3

Germany A1–D2
Graz E4
Grossglockner C4

Hohe Tauern
    Mountains
    C3–D4
Hungary F3–F5

Innsbruck B3
Italy A4–D5

Lake Constance A3
Liechtenstein
    A3–A4

Linz D2
Lower Austria
    (state) E2–F3

Mur River D4–E3

Neusiedler Lake F3
Niedere Tauern
    Mountains D3

Salzach River
    C2–C3
Salzburg (city) C3
Salzburg (state)
    C3–D4
Salzkammergut D3
Slovakia F2–F3
Slovenia D4–F4
Styria D3–F4
Switzerland A3–A5

Telfs B3
Tyrol A3–C4

Upper Austria
    (state) C2–E2

Vienna (city) F2
Vienna (state) F2
Vorarlberg (state)
    A3–A4

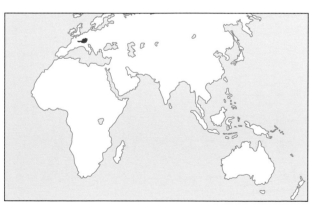

Quick Facts

Official name   Republic of Austria

Capital   Vienna

Official Language   German

Population   8,174,762 (July 2004 estimate)

Land Area   32,377 square miles (83, 857 square km)

States   Burgenland, Carinthia, Lower Austria, Salzburg, Styria, Tyrol, Upper Austria, Vienna, Vorarlberg

Highest Point   Grossglockner 12,461 feet (3,798 m)

Lowest Point   Neusiedler Lake 377 feet (115 m) above sea level

Border Countries   Czech Republic, Germany, Hungary, Italy, Liechtenstein, Slovakia, Slovenia, Switzerland

Major River   Danube

Major Lakes   Lake Constance, Neusiedler Lake

Major Cities   Graz, Innsbruck, Linz, Salzburg, Vienna

Major Religions   Roman Catholic, Protestant, Muslim, other

Currency   Euro (0.767 Euro = U.S. $1 in January 2005)

Opposite: This carved tree stump is in the Salzkammergut region, a popular vacation area.

Glossary

avalanches: snow, ice, or dirt that slides down the sides of mountains in a rush.

baroque: a style of architecture that uses very fancy, flowery designs.

cathedrals: important or large churches that often have lots of decorations.

chancellor: a high government official.

composers: people who write music.

concentration camps: camps in which people are kept prisoner.

culture: the customs, beliefs, language, literature, and art belonging to one group of people or to a country.

democratic: regarding a government in which the country's citizens can lead and can elect their leaders by vote.

dynasty: a series of rulers who rule over a long time and are from one family.

emperor: a person who rules an empire, which is a large collection of lands.

exported (v): sold and shipped from one country to another country.

federal: relating to a form of government in which separate states are all joined under one central government.

governor: a person who is elected to be the head of a region or state.

heir: someone who will receive a royal title or valuables when a person dies.

hydroelectric: regarding electricity that is produced when water passes through a dam and into a river below.

memorial: something built or done to help remember a person or event.

minerals: materials from the ground, such as rocks or salts, that are not made of animals or plants.

operas: plays that are usually performed along with the music of an orchestra and in which most words are sung.

parliament: a government group that makes the laws for their country.

republic: a country in which citizens elect their own lawmakers.

reserves: lands set aside so that animals and plants can survive there.

symphonies: long pieces of music that are written for an orchestra to play.

traditional: regarding customs or styles passed down through the generations.

United Nations: an international group that helps promote understanding and peace and also helps nations develop.

vocational: related to a job, profession, or skilled trade.

More Books to Read

Cooking the Austrian Way. Easy Menu Ethnic Cookbooks series. Helga Hughes (Lerner)

The Farewell Symphony. Anna Harwell Celenza (Charlesbridge Publishing)

Lipizzans. Lynn M. Stone (Rourke)

Look What Came From Austria. Look What Came From series. Kevin A. Davis (Franklin Watts)

The *Night Crossing.* Karen Ackerman (Random House)

Silent Night, Holy Night: The Story Behind Our Favorite Christmas Carol. Traditions of Faith series. Myrna Strasser (Zondervan)

Vienna. Cities of the World series. R. Conrad Stein (Children's Press)

Wolfgang Amadeus Mozart. Tell Me about series. John Malam (Carolrhoda Books)

Videos

Austria: Vienna and the Danube, Salzburg and the Lake District. Travel the World series. (Questar)

Exploring Austria and Germany. (SJB Productions)

Mozart's Austria. Armchair European Travel series. (Shade Tree Studios)

Strauss: The King of Three-Quarter Time. (Sony Classics)

Web Sites

www.artsalive.ca/en/mus/
greatcomposers/mozart/
mozart.html

www.californiamall.com/
holidaytraditions/traditions-
austria.htm

Due to the dynamic nature of the Internet, some web sites stay current longer than others. To find additional web sites, use a reliable search engine with one or more of the following keywords to help you locate information about Austria. Keywords: *Alps, Habsburgs, Danube, Haydn, Mozart, Salzburg, Vienna, waltz.*

Index